The Case of the Anonymous Donor

By
Ruth Bawell

CW00954341

Table of Contents

Unsolicited Testimonials

By **Phyllis**

⭐⭐⭐⭐⭐ **Love Ruth!**

I love Ruth's books! Her mysteries are the best!

⭐⭐⭐⭐⭐ **Love This Author**

Ruth Bawell is very creative and a great writer! All her books have left me unable to stop reading till the ending! There were a few Amish fact mistakes, like unmarried man having a beard, but the plot was so good I overlooked that!

By **Steve M**

⭐⭐⭐⭐⭐ **I love romance stories** August 5, 2017
I love romance stories... well written with her usual twists to the story still enjoyed them very much Once I start I can't put it down.

By **Bones**

⭐⭐⭐⭐⭐ **Amish County Stories**
I love all the Amish County stories! Each one brings so much excitement! Ruth Bawell is also a wonderful writer!

By **Kindle Customer**

⭐⭐⭐⭐⭐ **Good clean writing.**
The Amish stories of Ruth Bawell are authentic, faith-filled writings. They are short, more the length of novellas or longer short stories. Always clean, always uplifting.

FREE GIFT

Just to say thanks for checking our works we like to gift you

Our Exclusive Never Before Released Books

100% FREE!

Please GO TO

`http://cleanromancepublishing.com/gift`

And get your FREE gift

Thanks for being such a wonderful client.

Chapter One

"Well, it is a pleasure to talk with you today, Mrs. King and Mrs. Fisher. You must feel so proud of all you've accomplished these past couple of years," the young woman on the other end of the phone said with a cheerful tone.

Hannah shifted in her seat and looked at her friend on the settee beside her. "I don't know that I would say pride is the right word," Hannah replied.

"You must remember, Amish and Mennonites believe in humility. We are not prideful," Susan explained, and the interviewer on the other end of the line whistled.

"That is a lovely approach to life. My guests are usually quite proud of their accomplishments, especially when they involve murder," she said. Hannah gulped and leaned back in her seat, her eyes on Daniel, the young man helping them manage their microphones and all the tech equipment he'd brought into Susan's little bed and breakfast earlier in the day.

Hannah hadn't realized how much would be involved in joining a radio show as a guest. She'd thought they would talk on the phone with the hostess, a sleuthing enthusiast named Nancy Schmancy.

Hannah still thought the name was foolish, especially after being told it was a fake name the young woman used. Why in the world anyone would choose such a silly name was beyond her.

Daniel, a thirty-year-old man helping Hannah's business and Susan's with their social media outreach—a concept Hannah had never endeavored to understand—smiled. Then, he motioned for the microphone, reminding Hannah that she was supposed to be talking. They had been approached some week ago by Miss Schmancy to join her on her radio show which dealt with amateur sleuths around America. Hannah had reluctantly agreed after some convincing by Susan, who thought it would be a good opportunity for their businesses.

She leaned forward until her chin bumped into the large black microphone, and Susan pushed her back with a chuckle. "It wasn't a murder," she said cautiously, remembering the case involving the dead blogger on the beach. "The young woman drowned rather unfortunately while...erm..."

"Caving," Susan added with some delight at remembering the strange term.

"That's right," Hannah agreed. The voice from the large black box that had boomed whenever their hostess spoke came again.

"Well, yes. But there was some concern about a murderer on the loose, wasn't there? Your fiancée was a suspect, wasn't he?" There was no malice in Nancy's voice, but Hannah still felt her heart thundering at the question. She'd known it was coming. Daniel had spoken with Miss Schmancy and agreed on questions, but she'd dreaded it.

"Well, he was but only briefly. We were able to prove that it was all an accident," she quickly said.

"Ah, yes, you did. Given your strict faith, do you think God is sending you these cases to solve?"

Hannah looked at Susan, who leaned forward and cleared her throat. "I don't know. The Lord's ways are mysterious. All we can do is trust that he will guide us right."

"That's right," Hannah agreed quietly. Nancy did not miss a beat and swiftly moved on.

"Well, let's take some more calls, or shall we?" Nancy said, and Hannah could almost hear the speaker's smile.

They had already taken a few callers before, and when Hannah agreed to this interview, that scared her the most. They had been able to tell Nancy the questions they wanted to be asked, but the callers and their questions had been unknown. Hannah was pleasantly surprised as everyone was very nice and kind and asked interesting questions about the cases she had previously solved and the Amish community.

However, she had hoped that they would not have time for another round, but it seemed that hope had been misplaced. She glanced at the cuckoo clock in the corner and saw they had another fifteen minutes left.

"Oh sure," Susan said, who, unlike Hannah, had no qualms whatsoever about talking to strangers on the phone. On the contrary, she seemed to enjoy it.

"Very good!" Nancy cooed, and Hannah heard the clicking that indicated a caller was on the line.

"Who do we have?" Nancy asked cheerfully.

The voice of a young girl came down the line next, and Hannah smiled. They hadn't had any children calling in before.

"Hey, Mrs. King and Mrs. Fisher," the voice said, and Hannah frowned.

The voice was oddly familiar, but she couldn't quite place it. "I want to ask about Hoppy. How is Hoppy?"

Hannah smiled as she recognized the person speaking.

"Pauley, is that you?"

It had been some time since she had spoken to Pauley and Amy Bailey, Amanda's younger sisters. They lived in Sarasota, not very far from Pinecraft, but they did not come to visit them; perhaps that was for the best. Isaac and Amanda's relationship had been difficult for both families, and for the time being, distance appeared best. Still, Hannah could not help and wonder if they weren't just pushing out the inevitable. Because when Isaac had been in crisis over the revelation that his mother had not died in a drowning accident as he thought, but rather that her body had never been found, he turned to Amanda.

"Can I ask who's on the line?" Nancy asked, and Pauley chuckled. "Pauley Bailey. Mrs. King helped my sister Amy, me, and some of our Amish friends out when we got in trouble for hiding a few dogs."

Nancy broke into loud laughter that echoed out of the speakers. Daniel had set up Susan's living room so they could join the radio show. He had wanted them to wear headphones, but hearing the shrill laughter down the line made Hannah thankful that they had declined. She had put on the headphones but found them so oppressive and claustrophobic that she had to throw them to the side.

While she had opened her life to the English world and its customs in ways that some in the community found uncomfortable, there were some things she never wanted to do. Wearing headphones was among them.

"That's right," Nancy exclaimed as if she had just remembered an old friend. "The kidnapped dog caper. That was one of my favorite cases of all I have heard, Mrs. King. To our listeners who do not remember, a string of bizarre robberies hit Pinecraft about two years ago. Mrs. King found out in the end that the culprits were none other than the children of her friend Mrs. Gerber and the children of some of her guests. The reason for the robberies turned out to be something rather precious; they were hiding a pregnant dog and her mate. You adopted one of the puppies, didn't you, Mrs. King?"

Hannah beamed and glanced out into the lanai, where Jacob, the man whom she was soon wed, was seated on one-of Susan's rocking chairs. Hoppy, now a dog of ninety pounds, lay on the floor, his right side pressed against the window while the air conditioning from the window unit blew on him.

"I did. Hoppy. He's played a role in several of our investigations." She chuckled as she thought of the adventures the dog had come on with her. Of course, it was entirely against Amish customs to keep a pet, but Hoppy was so much more than that.

"Indeed, he was the star of one of them," Susan chimed in.

Nancy giggled. "Yes, the infamous dog-napping incident."

Hannah frowned and shook her head a little. It still appeared quite bizarre to her that her and Susan's adventures, and those she had shared with all of her friends, had spread beyond the borders of Pinecraft. But, if Daniel was to be believed, their stories were spread far and wide on the interwebs. Internuts… Whatever it was called.

That was how they had found themselves on this radio show in the first place. However, Daniel hadn't called it a radio show but something else. A pod something or other. A potblast? She couldn't quite recall.

Nancy Schmancy continued her chatter unabated. "Well, I wish I were there in person to meet him rather than here in chilly. Georgia. Although, of course, you've had a mystery or two to solve up here. Tell me, Hannah, do you ever plan on stopping solving mysteries?"

"Never!" Pauley shouted it down the phone, and Hannah realized that the little girl was still on the line.

"Well, I'm sorry, Pauley, but I have to disagree. I will stop solving mysteries just as soon as they stop finding me," Hannah replied kindly.

"You might have to move back to Ohio like Sarah and Noah for that," Susan said, and suddenly Hannah's smile faded a little. Her friends Noah and Sarah Peterheim had announced a few weeks ago that they would return to their former home in rural Ohio to live in a long- and old-ordered Amish community.

Well, it was Noah's home community. Sarah had been born and raised somewhere near Boston, if she remembered correctly. Still, since converting, Hannah had watched Sarah grow rather pious. Then, Sarah had confided that that was her wish a few weeks prior.

Hannah had difficulty accepting this change, as she was fond of not just the young couple but their little girl. However, given the many changes that were taking place in Pinecraft at the moment, she couldn't necessarily blame them.

She swallowed and looked down at her hands. The rooms were neat, but no wonder as she had spent an hour cleaning them earlier after tending to the garden with Noah and Jacob for most of the morning. She chewed her bottom lip and engaged in an activity that some of her English friends cheerfully referred to as zoning out.

The truth was she felt awful about the changes that were taking place in Pinecraft. A certain portion of her neighbors had made it known that they did not appreciate how Pinecraft had opened up to the English world of late. Instead, they wanted to return to a more secluded state.

The driving force behind this happening had been a particular gentleman who had moved into town not long ago. He had managed to dispose of the former deacon before departing town after decrying it far too open for his liking. But, while he was gone, the seeds he had planted had taken root, and there was now a small but loud portion of neighbors who lobbied for a closed society.

She knew Noah and Sarah's departure did not necessarily have to do with this movement. However, the ill treatment Sarah, a convert to their faith, had received had given them the final push. This would be their last season, and they would move away come January. Hannah knew this was almost a year away, but she still dreaded it.

Likewise, she dreaded Isaac losing his closest friends in the community. He had not made many friends in Pinecraft since his return from his rumspringa. His closeness to Amanda Bailey had marred his connection with the community. They accepted him, and many even liked him, but there had been a thin veil of separation between him and the rest of the community.

His friendship and residency at the home of Sarah and Noah had helped establish him a little more, but Hannah feared that without them, he'd lost his anchors. While he and Jacob were again close, a sense of unease remained—the sort that would perhaps take years to recover from.

"One more?" Nancy asked, and Hannah looked up. For a moment, she had a sense of not quite knowing where she was, so lost had she been in her thoughts.

Susan, on the other hand, was on a real roll. "Yes, I think we've got time for another one!" She was thoroughly cheerful as she rubbed her hands together.

"Alright then, let's go to one more caller. We have Ivan Leroy on the line. Ivan, what's shaking?" Nancy asked, and Hannah frowned as she was unfamiliar with that expression. She looked around to make sure there was not some sort of earthquake about to happen, but when she saw how relaxed Susan and Daniel were, she leaned back in her chair, dismissing the thought as silly.

However, she noted how her friend's eyebrows furrowed a little at the mention of the name, and then, when a deep, warm voice filled the space, Susan's shoulders grew tense.

"Well, hello, Nancy, Mrs. King, and Mrs. Fisher," the man said. His tone struck

Hannah as jolly and good-natured, but Susan's face grew pale.

"Hello," Hannah replied.

"Well, I just wanted to say that I am very fortunate to be moving to such a lovely place as Pinecraft," Mr. Leroy said.

"Oh, you're moving to Pinecraft? And from where, if I might ask?" Nancy inquired.

"Well, that is hard to say. I spent some time in Pennsylvania growing up. I'm from an Amish family, Pennsylvania Dutch to be exact, but we became Mennonite some decades ago and moved out of Lancaster County. Ended up in Ohio, then South Carolina." The man took a deep breath. "But before I give you my whole life's story, I should say I've been around the block. Now

I'm retired and looking forward to settling into Pinecraft."

"Well, we look forward to having you," Hannah said with a smile.

"When," Susan said, but her voice hitched, and she had to clear her throat. "When are you planning to move to Pinecraft?"

The man's reply was instantaneous.

"Oh, I just closed on a little house on Bikry Street near the Mennonite church. I'll be there this weekend."

Susan's lips turned into the shape of an O. "I see," she said and then chewed her bottom lip. Hannah had known Susan for decades and knew she only chewed her lip when she was severely distressed. But what about this man's statement could have distressed her? Was she worried he would join the faction of Amish who wanted to close off the community? But the man was Mennonite. The Mennonites had stayed out of the internal disagreement between the Amish.

"Well, isn't that lovely," Nancy said. "Always nice to have new neighbors. And maybe you'll get in on solving some mysteries with these ladies."

Mr. Leroy laughed at this. "I would not be opposed to that at all."

"Excuse me," Susan said suddenly and removed the tin microphone from her green blouse. She dropped it on the table and got up, the chair squeaking. Then, she rushed out of the room and out of The Nook.

As Hannah settled herself to ensure nobody on the radio noticed the disturbance, she realized—a new mystery might already be upon her. However, this one was a little more personal.

Chapter Two

"Hannah King, there you are," Mrs. Gerber trilled as she hurried across the street. She waved a piece of paper through the air as Hannah stopped outside Yoder's grocery store. Mr. Yoder, Mrs. Gerber's fiancée, peered out of his flower shop and smiled at Mrs. Gerber, who blushed. She stopped in front of Hannah, panting.

"Would you look at this," she said and waved the paper again. Upon closer inspection, Hannah recognized the item as a check. She took a step back, uncomfortable at the idea of looking at another person's financial affairs. However, Mrs. Gerber was determined for her to look at it. "Look, Hannah. Someone sent this to me as a gift. Can you believe it?"

"A gift," Hannah said rather reluctantly. It was one thing to sit together over a cup of coffee and share details about each other's lives; it was another to get into financial discussions. It was a topic she'd always avoided.

"Will you stop being difficult? I am attempting to share my joy with you."

A slight irritation entered her voice, and Hannah sighed, taking the check from her. She gasped when her eyes settled on the figure in the little box to the right.

"Five thousand dollars? Did someone send this to you? Who?" Hannah asked as she examined the check. It was a cashier's check, and there was no sender or memo line other than a gift.

"When did you receive this?" Hannah asked as she stared at the document.

"It came in the postbox this morning. I about had a heart attack when I opened it up. Can you believe it? Just an anonymous donor, it seems. A card with it said he'd heard we do good work in the community, and they wanted to help." She shrugged as she took the check back, folded it, and stuffed it into the pocket of her white apron. Hannah was about to make her alarm known because while they were a trusting community, one ought not to be so careless with money. However, she did not get the chance because Mr. Yoder stepped out of his shop.

"My dearest," he cooed as he walked past Hannah without acknowledging her. He gave Mrs. Gerber a peck on the cheek before looking at her check.

"Is that it?" he asked.

Mrs. Gerber nodded.

"It is, can you believe it? This is the card." She fished a plain blue card with a flower vase on the front out of her pink dress pocket. Mr. Yoder opened it and scratched his long white beard. "Very curious," he mused.

"You don't have a secret admirer, do you?" he teased, but Hannah detected a hint of jealousy in the older man's voice.

"I wish I had an admirer who sent me checks randomly, but I assure you, you are my only one. And we all know that your method of making your affections known doesn't involve checks." She giggled and looked at Hannah, who likewise grinned. "Instead, you trample flowers and blame goats."

Mr. Yoder grew red in the face. "I apologized time and again for that." He dropped his right hand and sighed heavily. "I'll never live it down."

Hannah shrugged. "Well, your courtship definitely started memorably. That is certain."

"I wonder who sent this," Mrs. Gerber said then, growing serious. "I wonder if anyone else received a gift."

Mr. Yoder looked at the card again. "Might be. Look here, Mrs. King, what does your sleuthing mind say?"

She took the card from him. There was no name, no signature, and the message was printed rather than written. It read simply:

I hope this helps you keep the Amish community of Pinecraft flourishing.

"If the sender wants to keep the community flourishing, I suppose there might be more gifts like this. I should speak to Deacon B..." She stopped and bit her lips, realizing that their deacon had departed Pinecraft.

After the revelation that Deacon Beiler had broken Amish custom by reconnecting with his shunned brother, he voluntarily left his position as a deacon. And while those who wanted to see him banished did not succeed in driving him away, his brother's sudden illness—a terminal condition only revealed after the commotion of the past few weeks—had called him away.

Pinecraft's Amish community was thus without a spiritual leader while the men quarreled for the position.

She lingered and chatted with Mrs. Gerber and Mr. Yoder for a few minutes longer and then bade them goodbye, returning home to her little inn, the strange donation fresh on her mind.

Hannah dropped her keys into the little wooden basket inside a private living room and then sat in the armchair beside Jacob. He patted her hand and smiled.

"I thought you were heading out to fetch a pint of milk. You were gone for quite some time."

Hannah shrugged. "Can you believe that I forgot about the milk?" She shook her head. "I was distracted by Mrs. Gerber. She flagged me down because she received an anonymous donation."

Jacob turned around, his red lips slightly parted.

"A donation? Was it an anonymous check in an envelope saying something about doing good things for the community?"

Hannah slipped to the edge of her seat. "Yes. How do you know?

He leaned back. "I stopped by Mrs. Pendergast's house to help her fix her gate. She told me her brother, Abraham, who has the tricycle repair shop, received a check for two thousand dollars in the mail yesterday, saying it was for all the good work he has done during the hurricane, you know, repairing everybody's bicycles and such."

Hannah chewed her bottom lip. "Says so? So two people in the community have received anonymous donations. Who could be doing such a thing? Not that I'm questioning anybody's intentions."

Jacob crossed his legs as he sat back.

"Well, whoever it is, he seems to know the area well enough to know that Mr. Pendergast has done a lot to give back to our community, and so has Mrs. Gerber."

Hannah tipped her head to one side. She did not want to be unkind, but she could not remember what grand community project her friend had undertaken as of late. Then, as if he were reading her mind, Jacob smiled. "I think the anonymous donor was speaking about Mrs. Gerber's sewing circle."

Hannah sucked in a gulp of air, chiding herself for having forgotten this wonderful project her friend had founded. The year prior, Mrs. Gerber, in response to the horrible hurricane that had swept through Sarasota, decided to found what she called a sewing circle.

Women from the community, Amish and English alike, came together once a month and spent an afternoon making blankets, towels, and pillowcases. The meetings had been held once a week during the season when there were more people in town. The project started as a community effort to help the people who had lost everything replace their belongings.

But since then, it had merged into a project-driven venture. At the moment, the group was making blankets for the Salvation Army homeless shelter. Before that, they had worked together on doilies and onesies for a project for young mothers.

It was a lovely, worthwhile project, and she was very happy to help when she had the chance. She was not skilled at quilting or sewing, but she did what she could and appreciated her efforts.

"I suppose those are both very good community efforts. I just wonder who our benefactor is and who might be next."

Jacob chuckled. "Are you going to turn that into a case for Hannah King? Or are you thoroughly occupied with your other project?"

It took Hannah a moment to realize what he was talking about, and then she shook her head and giggled.

"Oh, that. I will say that wanting to find out why Susan was so upset at the radio show is more of personal curiosity. She doesn't usually act like that. She's been acting like her usual self for the last few days, but whenever I mentioned the radio show, she grew grumpy. Thus, I haven't had a chance to even talk to her much about the matter."

"Do you think it has something to do with the caller—that Ivan fellow?" Jacob mused.

Hannah shrugged. "I really can't say. But she was perfectly jolly before then."

"She's not one prone to foul moods, not like some people we know," he said and nodded his chin toward Leah, Hannah's sister, who was presently quarreling with her husband Lucas in the garden. Hannah's sister had mellowed some over the years, but she'd never quite lost her cantankerous attitude.

"Well, that is true. It is strange. I wish she would talk to me," Hannah sighed as Hoppy toddled out of the lanai and into the room, flopping down in front of her as he did. The dog was massive now, and the weight and warmth of his body always made Hannah feel comforted.

"We will find out in time, I reckon," Jacob concluded the subject. "Say, you haven't seen Isaac, have you?"

Hannah wet her lips and shook her head. "No, not today. I saw him yesterday as I was walking back from The Nook. He was just heading into the bakery. We talked a little but he didn't have a whole lot to say. He was tired from work."

Isaac presently helped both at the bakery and also at the flower shop in addition to helping his father with repairs around the town. Usually they saw Isaac several times a day as he lived so close, but she hadn't spotted the young man as regularly these past few days.

"Always busy, my boy," Jacob sighed, then leaned back and picked up the leather-bound bible he'd been reading earlier. Hannah settled beside him, one hand on his leg while Hoppy snored at her feet. She would not make too much of Susan's behaviors, she decided. Instead she would enjoy this evening with her dear Jacob. Peace and quiet were a hot commodity to come by, and she'd learned to cherish it when she had it.

Chapter Three

Three days later, on a pleasant Saturday morning, Hannah and Susan were walking toward Flinders, a new restaurant they had wanted to try, offering Pennsylvania Dutch breakfast foods. Jacob peddled his tricycle beside them, sharing in the latest news of the anonymous donor.

"One arrived at the *Voll Schpass Kinder Circle*, and then the Peterheims' got one as well. Just arrived in the mail yesterday. The same kind of letter and card, can you believe it?" Hannah said as she and Susan were walking down Beneva Road.

Susan looked dubious. "It is rather odd, wouldn't you say? It must be someone who's after something, don't you think?"

Hannah frowned. "I hope not. I'd like to think of this as just a kind soul looking to do something good for like-minded people."

Jacob chuckled. "Our Susan; she's grown into a proper pessimist."

"I will remind you that I am one of the most optimistic people in all of Pinecraft. I cannot help that so many rotten people are walking this earth. Just look at what happened in your community with poor Deacon Baylor being chased out. It was rotten. Rotten I say."

Hannah took a deep breath. "I can't deny that there has been a change in the air. It's regrettable, really." She nodded her chin toward the bakery. "It'll feel a little less bright once Noah and Sarah are gone."

Jacob, who had been slowly peddling alongside them, slowed down further. When his eyes met Hannah's, she saw in them the worry that had plagued him ever since finding out that his son's good friends were leaving. "I worry so much about what's going to happen to Isaac. He'll be so lonely."

Susan shook her head. "I should think he'll be just fine. He's doing quite well with his community project, isn't he?"

Hannah and Jacob exchanged a glance.

"Community project?" Jacob asked

Susan frowned a little and then nodded. "Why yes. I saw him at the bus stop a week ago and asked him where he was headed. He said he had spearheaded a project to clean up the parks of Sarasota, and he was meeting with a few other volunteers. I've seen him get on the bus plenty of times this week. You know the bus stop is just outside my office, right?"

Hannah took a deep breath. This was not the type of news she had been looking for. Because if Isaac had been involved in the community project, he certainly hadn't told her about it. And he usually told her everything. Or so she had thought.

Jacob tipped his head to one side. "I wonder what that project is about. And if they might need more volunteers. I have a mind to ride down to the bakery and ask."

"No, Jacob, don't do that. The boy will think that you're checking up on him."

Jacob winked at her. "Well, I am. Aren't I?"

Then he drove away, whistling as he did. However, Hannah knew that that was a pretense to allow Susan to think everything was all right. Hannah and Susan were close, but when it came to Isaac, she and Jacob had long agreed that they would not involve the friends and families. Too fragile was the young man's disposition, to fresh the trauma that almost tore him apart.

Fortunately for Hannah, and perhaps unfortunately so for Susan, they were swiftly distracted by a large blue-and-yellow moving truck that came down the street in front of them. Hannah turned her head to the right and followed the vehicle as it turned onto Birky Street.

"Why, I wonder if that is that gentleman from the radio. He said he was moving into the area this week."

A small nondescript white car followed behind the moving truck and stopped in front of one of the little bungalows.

Hannah stopped. She had a mind to say hello to the new arrival to make them feel comfortable in Pinecraft, but Susan had other ideas.

"Hannah, come on, let's go. I'm in no mood to meet some stranger."

"That's not very neighborly of you. The Nook is just down the street as well. You're going to see this gentleman sooner or later. He sounds awfully interested in our community, and he's Mennonite. All the more reason that you should introduce yourself. Maybe give him the schedule for your church."

Susan cringed as the car's passenger side door opened, and a man exited. He was dressed in a beige pair of pants, black loafers, and a button-down white shirt over which he wore a cardigan that was open in the front.

His face was clean-shaven, and his hair, a dark blonde, hung in a shaggy manner down underneath a hat. He wasn't wearing the straw hat common amongst Amish or even Mennonite men. Instead, he wore a black fedora with a little flower sticking up.

Hannah was about to walk over and introduce herself when the driver's side door opened, and the woman stepped out. She was much younger than the man, who was closer to Susan and Hannah's age. The young woman appeared young enough to be his daughter.

Hannah turned to her friend with a broad smile. "We should say hello."

"No," Susan replied, in a rather harsh tone. "I don't think so. We don't even know if he is the man who called the radio show."

"Who else could it be? He's moving onto Birky street. There are but ten houses on the street," Hannah protested.

"If you must say hello, by all means do so, but don't pull me into your scheme," Susan replied and marched off. Hannah stood for a moment, utterly confused. Then, she glanced at the man standing not far from her with the young woman. He'd looked over his shoulder and watched the exchange, she realized.

Hannah felt heat rising to her cheeks. Unsure what to do, she raised her hand and waved. The man, who she was sure was Ivan Leroy, raised his in turn and nodded. The young woman, who upon closer inspection did look just like him, did likewise.

Hannah pondered what to do and looked after Susan when a sigh escaped her. Hannah could not make sense of her friend acting rather odd. Leaving Mr. Leroy behind, she rushed after her.

"Susan, what has gotten into you? You're not usually so rude," Hannah chided Susan, who stopped in her tracks and spun around.

"Rude? I am rude because I don't want to accost a stranger in the street?" Her cheeks were red, and her eyes were wide as she glared at Hannah.

"Accost? I wanted to say hello, that's all," Hannah defended herself, utterly shocked.

"Hannah, I don't want to talk about it anymore. I have to go. I have a dentist appointment," Susan declared, much to Hannah's confusion.

"Dentist? It's Saturday! And we were going to Flinders for lunch."

Her friend pursed her lips and shrugged. "I must have forgotten. But I have an appointment. They are open on Saturday, you know. I have to go. See you later, Hannah."

She rushed away, leaving Hannah to stand there, utterly confused. She knew of no dentist that was open on Saturdays and Susan hadn't complained of any dental troubles. It was all rather curious. She looked back once more to see Mr. Leroy enter the small, white house with the stark yellow fence and disappear inside.

Something about this man had rattled her friend. The question was—what?

Chapter Four

"That doesn't sound like her, Hannah," Jacob said when they spoke the following afternoon. "Something must be going on. Does she know Mr. Leroy?"

Hannah shook her head. "I don't think so. She didn't mention it. It is so strange. She acted that way when she heard his voice on the radio, though, so I feel she must know him..." She scratched her chin when the front door opened, then peered out and saw two men with bags entering.

"Welcome to the Restful Traveler Inn," Esther trilled. "Rabbi Wise, Mrs. Easton."

Hannah smiled as she recognized both the names. They were repeat guests, just like so many of her clients. Usually, she would have gone outside to greet them herself, but her mind was too occupied with her quarrel with Susan.

A familiar voice joined when the door chimed for a second time, and Jacob looked up.

"Isaac?" he called, and a moment later, his son poked his head around the corner and smiled.

"Well, there you are. How are you?" he asked and smiled at Hannah before settling his eyes on his father. Hannah smiled at the young man who would be her stepson soon enough though she could not help but think back to the secret he'd been keeping.

"We're enjoying this lovely Sunday afternoon. What of you, son? I came to look for you yesterday, but Sarah said you'd gone out early. That community project keeping you busy?"

Isaac's eyes widened a fraction, but then he cleared his throat.

"Oh, yes. I didn't mention it because I only just started. It's going well," he said, but Hannah noticed that he wasn't meeting their eyes.

"What is it? Cleaning parks? Sounds like a worthwhile effort. I'd be interested in helping out," Hannah said by way of gathering more information.

Isaac ran his tongue over his lips and shrugged. "I don't know, Hannah. It's pretty labor-intensive. Picking up garbage and such."

"Are you saying I'm too old? I'll have you know I replanted the entire garden almost on my own without any help, and you know we all helped out with clean up after the hurricane," she said, only slightly offended. She knew well that in the eyes of a young one like Isaac, she was an old woman. Perhaps in the eyes of most people…

"Anyway, it's for the young kids, you know. High school and such," Isaac said. "I didn't have anything to do with recruitment. I just help out."

"I thought you told Mrs. Fisher you spearheaded the project," Jacob said, but there was caution in his voice. They both knew that Isaac was jumpy and always had been since the events of the past year.

Isaac ran one hand through his hair and shrugged. "I suppose I was a little boastful. I wanted to sound as though I was accomplishing things, I guess. It's not like I have much to show off otherwise."

"Life is not about showing off," Jacob reminded his son. "Life is about doing good, being good, and doing the Lord's work. And you certainly are." Jacob had meant the words to encourage, Hannah knew this, but Isaac shifted his weight as though he were not entirely pleased with the statement, as though it made him uncomfortable.

"Well, anyway. Any news on the person sending checks to people?" Isaac asked, changing the conversation.

Hannah shook her head. "No, nothing new as to who it is. Though another check arrived today at Yoder's. Specifically it was a check with a notation that flowers should be sent to the Stoltzfus' nursing home for the old people. There was enough money to send flowers for the entire year, every Wednesday."

The Stoltzfus couple had founded a nursing home that catered to Amish and Mennonite people, though it was open to all. Hannah sometimes volunteered at the facility and she knew that a few flowers would surely spruce up the place a great deal.

Isaac smiled. "That's nice. It seems there are a few good people left in the world. I hope we get to find out who it is so we can thank them properly."

"Perhaps it's that new fellow, Leroy," Jacob said, only half jesting.

"The one Mrs. Fisher dislikes so much?" Isaac asked. When Hannah frowned, he elaborated. "She told me about it at the bus stop the other day. Said that he should be ashamed of himself, showing up here with a girlfriend young enough to be his daughter. I mentioned that maybe she is his daughter, but she would not hear of it."

Hannah chuckled. It was just like Susan to jump to such conclusions.

"She looks as much like him as you look like your father, so I think you might be right," Hannah said and Jacob chuckled.

"Well, there's no denying we are kin, is there, Isaac?"

The two men nodded at one another, smiles on their lips. Hannah would have relaxed at the sight of this, but there was something odd about Isaac. She wasn't quite sure what it was, but she had a feeling that all was not as well as he'd have them believe.

As for Mr. Leroy, Hannah had vowed to herself to let the new arrival settle into town before investigating just why her friend disliked him so much. But now that she'd heard the latest, she was determined to find out exactly what was going on. She only had to find a good time to converse with him without being obvious about it.

It wasn't godly to be curious or stick your nose into other people's business, but she knew that when it came to Susan and this man, something was amiss. She wanted to find out just what it was, because if it troubled Susan so much, she had to step in and help. And if soothing her curiosity was a side effect, then she would certainly welcome it.

Chapter Five

It wasn't until two days later that Hannah finally had a chance to introduce herself properly to the new arrival.

She had gone into Peterheims' bakery and retrieved several loads of bread for her guests when she saw the man walking out of his house on Birky Street. She hadn't been sure whether she should wave to him or say anything at all, but as it turned out, she didn't have to worry.

"Mrs. King! It's so nice to see you again. I thought of coming up to you and just knocking on the door of the Restful Traveler, seeing how we had already conversed on the radio, but I wasn't sure. I figured it might be seen as improper by your fiancé." He looked past her as though he were searching for something, or rather, someone

"All alone today?" he asked.

Hannah smiled. "Jacob is not with me. But I feel that is not who you were asking me about."

He shrugged. "I had hoped to run into your friend Mrs. Fisher. But it seems she is rather intent on avoiding me."

Hannah grimaced. She had hoped that Mr. Leroy had not seen them the day he had moved in, although it had appeared rather apparent that he had.

"I don't think she's avoiding you. She's usually a very open-hearted person, the first to welcome newcomers into town. She's just been a little under the weather."

This was not strictly speaking a lie. Susan hadn't acted like her usual self lately, and being under the weather was as likely an explanation as any. At least Hannah told herself that.

"That's so? I've always known her to be in rather robust health."

Hannah pursed to lips. "So you know her. Beyond just what you heard and read about her and me?"

He nodded. "She and I met some years ago. I was staying in South Carolina with some distant Mennonite relatives of mine, and she was there for similar reasons. It was just after her husband passed away. I take it she hasn't mentioned it."

Hannah rubbed her lips together. "I am afraid Mrs. Fisher and I, that's to say, my husband, who died, and I had a falling out with her and Mr. Fisher. My late husband and I were close friends with Susan and her late husband, but there was a disagreement… It doesn't matter. The truth is we did not speak to each other for many, many years. We conversed briefly after her husband passed as I wanted to give her my condolences, but after that, she went away to visit her son in South Carolina and did not return for almost a year."

"Yes, her son. Nice fellow. The whole family is quite nice. I had the pleasure of dining with them a few times." His smile told Hannah that he knew Susan's family much better than just in passing.

"It's a shame that you didn't keep in touch. But I suppose that's what it is like. Sometimes we make friends with people while on vacation, and when the vacation ends, so does the friendship. I see it all the time in my profession."

His smile faded, and he stuffed his hands in his pockets.

"I suppose that is one way of saying it. She really never did mention me, did she?"

Hannah had trouble meeting his eye because she could tell from the tone in his voice that he desperately wanted her to say that Susan had mentioned him. But the truth was she never did.

"I am sorry, but she didn't. I do not mean to intrude into your personal business, Mr. Leroy."

He waved a hand. "I think I have said enough already for you to understand that I was very fond of your friend. And I thought she was of me. However, things... Well. You know. I suppose, in a way, I ought to be grateful to have had a pleasant summer with her. It is more than I thought I'd ever have after burying my darling Ruth."

Hannah nodded solemnly. "I can understand that. I felt the same with my Elijah. After he passed, I thought that I'd be alone for all my days. But then the Lord saw fit to bring Jacob into my life." She looked up at the man's understanding eyes. "I am sorry it was not the same for you. I would have liked…"

She stopped mid-sentence as a thought came to her.

"It is not because of Susan that you are here?" The idea alarmed her, but to her relief, the man chuckled.

"No, not at all. My daughter, Hester, lives here. She moved here after meeting Susan years ago. Susan raved about Sarasota so much that Hester decided to visit, and then she ended up staying. I would never stalk Susan. I… The truth is, she is the reason I did not move here sooner. I didn't want her to think I was following her."

Hannah listened carefully, trying to comprehend all of this. Their widowhood was something she and Susan had in common, though even the loss of their beloved husbands had not managed to bridge the gap between the two of them. It had taken several more years after losing their husbands before they would be friends once more.

And this was the first time Hannah had heard that there had been somebody Susan might have been interested in.

"I am glad to hear it. And I hope that her cold reaction to your presence here won't deter you from making your mark here among us."

"Not to worry. I think Susan was just surprised at my being here, and perhaps she feels like you did, that I came because of her. Perhaps, if you'd be so kind, you could tell her that is not so? That I have no intention of bothering her?"

Hannah nodded, determined to make this unfortunate incident go away. Hopefully, once Susan knew the gentleman had no ill intentions, she'd feel better about his presence here. At least, that was her goal.

Chapter Six

Having bidden the gentleman farewell, Hannah immediately made her way to The Nook.

The bell above The Nook's front door chimed, and Daniel's face appeared behind the counter a second later.

"Mrs. King, I was about to head over to your place next. I've got to upload an update, and I think your printer drivers also need to be looked at."

Hannah shrugged. "Whatever it is you need to do. Where is Susan?"

He nodded towards the back where Susan's office was located.

Hannah passed the young man, who looked at her, puzzled. No wonder. Usually, Hannah always engaged in lively banter with him when it came to his tech talk. Today, however, she had other things on her mind.

"Hannah?" Susan said, swiftly followed by her nearly choking on her coffee at the surprise of seeing her friend.

"Is your mouth still numb from the dentist?" Hannah asked in what she was well aware was a snippy tone. As she walked towards Susan's place, a certain sense of anger had taken root in her. She and Susan had agreed to let bygones be bygones, and she had thought they were back on the same terms they had been before the friendship had been interrupted by a foolish argument about the property.

"I..." Susan looked away. Her faith was as opposed to lying as Hannah's. Therefore, she had known that her friend would not be able to continue the lie when directly confronted with it.

"It's all right. I already know that you didn't go to the dentist. I already know that you and Mr. Leroy know each other quite well. So there's no need to fib anymore."

Susan looked up. Her eyes grew wide. "Oh, Hannah. Did you have to go poking your nose where it doesn't belong again?"

"Again? I don't like the implication. I don't stick my nose where it doesn't belong. Anyway, I will let you know that you are quite wrong if you think this nice gentleman is here because of you."

Susan cringed. "Yes, I gathered that. Daniel helped me look up his daughter on Facebook, and I saw that she lives in Gulf Gate. She had some postings about convincing her father to come here."

"Right," Hannah said and crossed to arms. "So you see, he's not here because of you but because of his daughter. Although it seems she is here because of you."

Susan raised her eyebrows. "She is? We were never particularly close, so that does surprise me."

Hannah shrugged. "It seems your talk about our community impressed her so much that it brought her here. Anyway, why didn't you tell me who Mr. Leroy was when you called into the radio show? I knew something was wrong. You might as well have told me instead of lying and avoiding me."

It occurred to Hannah that she had no right to make demands of her friend. Hannah and Susan were close, but she didn't really have a right to know anything. Yet, knowing that her friend had been lying to her hurt.

Susan leaned back. "I wanted to, but the truth is I'm a little ashamed."

"Ashamed? But why?"

Susan looked to her right, where a picture of her and her late husband Benjamin was framed in a golden frame. A candle was lit in front of it the way it always was when Susan was alone in this room.

"After I lost my Benny, I felt I had lost an anchor. You and I had a falling out, and I didn't have you to turn to, so I went home. That is, to South Carolina, where my kids live. But you know that."

Hannah listened, a little unsettled because she did not like to think about their unfortunate years at each other's throats.

"Honestly, I thought that if I went home, everything would fall into place again. That I would feel settled, I would feel better. But I didn't. I went for long walks; you know the house is not far from the beach. That gave me some tranquility but not really. It wasn't until I met Ivan that things changed. His wife passed…"

Hannah nodded. "He mentioned that."

"Yes, she struggled with cancer, and it was a very difficult time for him. He needed someone to talk to, someone who could understand. And I could. And I needed the same."

Hannah took a deep breath and inhaled a strong whiff of rosemary that drifted out of the kitchen behind Susan's office. She understood all too well. After she lost her husband, she felt the same way, lost and alone. She'd been fortunate enough to have Leah, Lucas, and Esther around her and her business, which kept her busy. But still, she could understand all too well.

"We bonded over having lost our spouses as well as being Mennonites. We went to church together. Soon, we would meet for coffee before church, then we would add a walk after church. Before you knew it, we also met during the week to have lunch, to visit a museum... Soon enough, our friendship felt like more. It felt like too much."

Hannah ground her teeth as she listened and then wagged her head again. "I understand. I felt the same when I met Jacob. I thought about my feelings for him for a very long time because I thought that it wasn't right. I didn't deserve to find happiness again."

"But keep in mind that you met Jacob years after your husband died. I met Ivan six months after. I felt so guilty. He asked me to stay in South Carolina for a while to spend more time together. I had gotten to know his family; he had gotten to know mine. It would've been easy to stay, to pursue whatever it was between us, but I wasn't ready. I couldn't do it."

"So you left and came back here."

"I did. I threw myself into business, and before I knew it, a year had passed; then you and I made our peace, and now it has been more than three years since I last saw him. When I heard his voice on the radio, I knew it was him. And when I heard that he was coming here… He wrote to me once, a few months after I left. Confessing that he had fallen in love with me. He asked if he might come to visit but said if I didn't respond to the letter, he would take that as a no. I never replied and he never wrote again. I thought it was over."

"So when he suddenly showed up after all these years, you thought it was because of you," Hannah said gently.

"Of course I did. I didn't know his daughter lived here. I felt terrible because a part of me was happy to hear his voice and to see him. But another part still felt so guilty."

"Have you never thought that maybe it was a blessing?"

"A blessing?" Her friend's forehead fell into a deep frown.

"Yes, a blessing. That is how I came to see Jacob. He appeared in my life when I needed it the most, so I took it as a sign from the Lord that I wished to have love again. Perhaps it is the same for you. Especially now that so many years have passed."

"Oh, Hannah," Susan said, reaching across the desk to hold her hand. "I… I wanted to go up to him and talk to him. But I couldn't. It was all too much. And thought that he was here because of me…"

"He told me that you were the reason he didn't move here sooner. He didn't want to make you feel uncomfortable," Hannah said, finally relaying the message she had been tasked with,

"Did he really say so?"

"Yes. That's why I'm here. He asked me to tell you that. But, Susan, don't let this chance pass you by. At least see him for a cup of coffee. See if those sparks that you both remember are still there. And Benny would want you to be happy; you know that. I think you counseled me similarly when it came to Jacob."

Susan chuckled because it was true. "Oh, Hannah, I'm so glad you know now. I was wrong not to confide in you sooner."

"No, you are right. I guess I do stick my nose where it doesn't belong."

"Well, you do, but often with good results for those whose business you intrude on!"

The two women laughed, but then Susan looked past Hannah to the outside.

"Oh, I wonder if that's Isaac."

Hannah looked in the direction Susan had and spotted a bus making its way toward the bus stop.

"This is when I usually see him get off the bus," Susan elaborated.

Hannah nodded but did not take her eyes off the white-and-blue bus that had just pulled in. Then, she focused on the door and two very familiar figures behind it. She pushed her chair up, legs wobbling. "Susan, I'm sorry, but I have to go.

"Why? What happened," Susan asked, but Hannah had already turned and run out of The Nook and toward the bus.

Chapter Seven

She watched as the doors opened with their telltale beeping and hissing. Then, her mouth almost dropped open when Isaac stepped out, and beside him was none other than Amanda Bailey. Hannah immediately hurried toward where Isaac and Amanda were presently standing.

She walked at a brisk pace that caused her blue dress to swish around her legs. Her heavy leather shoes banged on the sidewalk as she closed the distance between herself and the two young people. She wanted to tell herself that they had met by accident. Perhaps Isaac had been going to volunteer, and Amanda just happened to be on the same bus, but it was clear from how they looked at one another that it was not so.

There was a distinct look in the way they stared at one another. A way that Susan liked to describe as lovey-dovey. She walked toward them, wondering just what Amanda was doing here to begin with. She was meant to be out of town, at school.

As she neared, Amanda looked up, and her face fell. She turned away and whispered a few words to Isaac, who glanced up at Hannah, and then Amanda rushed down the street.

This alarmed Hannah more than anything else because it was now quite clear that this was a clandestine meeting that nobody was ever supposed to know about. At least for now.

"Isaac. Isaac Troyer. What is this?"

Isaac stuffed his hands into his pockets and shuffled his feet.

"Oh, hi, Hannah," he said and smiled weakly.

"Do not 'Hi Hannah' me. That was Amanda. There's no use denying it."

He extracted one hand from his pocket and ran it through his blonde hair.

"Erm, well, yes." He let out a deep sigh. "I knew it was stupid to take the bus here. But her connection is here. It seemed foolish for her to wait for the next bus. You know how the buses are here in Sarasota? Next was not for an hour, and anyway, her classes started in half an hour and...." He stammered as he spoke, the words tumbling out one over the other in a rapid fashion.

"Classes? What are you talking about? Isn't she supposed to be up north?"

Isaac cringed and placed his hand on Hannah's elbow. "Do you mind if we sit?"

Hannah nodded and followed him across the street, further away from Pinecraft, where they sat on the bench inside a bus stop. Even though it was cooler outside now, the sun could still be quite harsh, and she appreciated his thoughtfulness in seeking shelter. What she didn't appreciate was being lied to.

"Well?" she demanded, eyes fixed on him. On the street before them, tricycles drove past, cars carefully weaving around them.

He gulped and his Adam's apple popped. "I had hoped not to share this with anyone just yet because I don't know what to do…"

"Isaac, start at the beginning. Why is Amanda not up north in school?"

He took a deep breath and looked at the ground where a piece of gum had been pressed into the concrete.

"She was, but her parents are getting divorced and… I don't know all the details, but it seems like her father has been in trouble. He lost a lot of the family's money, and her mother found out, and now they're getting divorced. He spent the rest of Amanda's college fund, and there isn't enough left for her to still go to school. She managed to transfer down here to go to an in-state school because it's cheaper. Anyway, we have kept in touch every now and again since I reached out to her. That's how I found out."

"I remember not too long ago, I asked you specifically if you were still in touch with her, and you told me you weren't." She could not keep the accusation out of her voice.

"I wasn't. Not back then. We didn't speak to each other for months. Not until she sent me a letter to tell me what happened with her family. I wrote back, and then the next time I heard from her, she was already back here. I just couldn't… She was so upset, and she didn't really have anyone to lean on. Her mother is angry, her sisters are so devastated, and she has to look after everyone. And nobody's looking after her. She needed someone. A friend." He shrugged and stroked the small beard that was growing on his chin. "So I met up with her."

"Are you and her… Is it…" Hannah didn't quite know what she wanted to ask, let alone how to formulate it.

Isaac rolled his shoulders forward. "I don't know, Hannah. I really don't know. If she were an Amish girl, I would've already proposed to her. But she's not. And I can't see her ever being one. She's what the Englisher called a feminist, not the sort to be able to enjoy a life of being a mother and wife. But at the same time, the truth is that when we are apart, I don't feel like I'm whole, you know?"

Hannah sat silently for a moment because the truth was she knew exactly how he felt. It had been the same when she was a young girl and first met her dearly departed husband. She felt like she was home with her husband at her side.

"When my Elijah passed away, I still felt a part of me died with him. I hadn't felt whole again till I met your father," she said quietly. She knew this was not what she should be telling this young man grappling with his faith, but it was the truth. "You already know what you're going to do, don't you?"

He closed his eyes. "I know what I want to do. I want to be with her, and if it means joining the world of Englisher, I will. But I also know what I don't want. I don't want to lose my family."

They both knew that the standard consequence for marrying someone who wasn't of their faith was to be shunned. But Hannah had seen just how much pain this practice caused, and she could not say that she fully supported it anymore. Especially not when it came to her child. Because even though she had not given birth to Isaac, she felt he was her child. To lose him would be devastating. And if she felt that way, how would Jacob feel?

"Your father, I don't know how he will take this. I don't know how he's going to recover."

"I know. That's why I haven't said anything. I keep thinking maybe one day I'll just wake up, and I won't feel this way anymore."

Hannah took a deep breath. "But it's been years since you've known her."

"Yes. And yet I feel the same. I think I always will."

Hannah looked left and right before turning to Isaac again. "Listen to me. You can't keep this a secret from your father. You need to tell him. As soon as possible. We cannot lie to him. You know yourself how painful that is."

He chewed his bottom lip before wagging his head in agreement.

"I'll tell him. Give me two weeks, please. Just so I can sort everything out in my head, talk to Amanda and all that. Please."

Hannah groaned under her breath. She did not want to keep this from Jacob for two weeks. "One week, that is all I'll agree to."

Isaac considered her for a moment as if trying to gauge how serious she was and then extended his hand to her. "A week. Alright. I'll do it."

"One more thing. There is no volunteer project, is there?"

He grimaced. "There is. I was involved in it, but I dropped out because of Amanda. I'm sorry I made it sound as if I was still part of it."

"Alright, alright. No more lies from now on. Agreed?"

They shook on it, and then, they parted ways, with Isaac making his way back to the bakery where he now lived and Hannah back to the inn. In the last couple of hours, she'd managed to solve two of the mysteries that had plagued her. One with a most positive outcome, and the other…. Well. Isaac's confession had rocked her, and she knew this was only the beginning. The moment he made his renewed connection to Amanda Bailey known, their life would be turned upside down. Again.

Chapter Eight

Hannah dropped her purse on the desk and stepped into the communal living room meant for their guests. As she stepped in, she saw Jacob seated at the table, her sister Leah beside him, and sitting with them was an older gentleman dressed in a black suit and a white shirt. On his head, he wore what she'd learned was a kippah.

"Good evening, Rabbi Wise," she said with a bright smile as she pulled up a chair. She didn't feel very jovial after speaking to Isaac, but the rabbi always had a way of making her feel at ease.

He was one of their biannual visitors. He was the head of a small Jewish congregation in Maine, but he came down to Sarasota frequently for visits. When he did, he usually chose to stay at the Restful Traveler Inn. Hannah did not know much about him since he seemed busy whenever he was in town, but she knew him to be a conscientious, kind-hearted man.

"Mrs. King," he said, "I had hoped to see you." She loved his pleasant New England accent.

"As did I. I knew you were arriving today. In fact, I saw you but hadn't expected you until the evening. I'd set aside some time this evening, but you got here early."

He nodded. "I took an early flight. Every time I book my flights, I tell myself, Eugene, I tell myself, you should get up earlier in the morning so you can take the early flight, and there's not such a rush to get to the temple in the evening on a Friday. So this time, I did." He let out a chuckle.

Hannah did not know much about his religion. Still, she had come to learn that on Friday nights, the rabbi always attended religious services at a synagogue nearby. In addition, she had learned that his religion had different levels of observance. While he was not the strictest, he preferred walking to his church rather than taking a car.

Of course, his church was not called the church but the synagogue, though he referred to it as a temple. Hannah briefly shook her head. Sometimes the customs and terminology of other religions were complicated for her

"I spoke to your young assistant, Rebecca, when I booked my stay here. What a pleasant young woman. I heard she's going to be a lawyer."

Hannah smiled at this. "Yes. I'm so glad you had a chance to meet her – at least over the phone. She went to Key West for a couple of weeks to visit family. Her aunt Ruth also works here, but she's in Key West too."

The rabbi smiled broadly. "That she also told me. I told her I hoped that next time I would be able to spend a little bit more time with her. My congregation sent volunteers down to Port-au-Prince after that awful earthquake they had there years ago. I was fortunate enough to be down there for two weeks. Such a strong people, such a tragedy. And yet, even at the darkest hour, I found the people down there to be so kind." He slapped his hand on the table. "But let us not speak of such sad, sad things anymore.

Jacob and Leah just told me that you were amidst a new mystery."

Hannah nodded. With so many mysteries on her hands, it was a miracle she knew exactly what he was talking about.

"Yes. It seems we have an anonymous donor."

She looked at Jacob and Leah, who cleared her throat. "I was about to tell the rabbi and Jacob the latest. I've just spoken to Mrs. Stadler. Do you remember she had been trying to start a little community project with the children? Taking them down to the beach and educating them on the wildlife?"

Jacob nodded. "Yes, but she's been looking to raise funds for the project. To bring in a few more people to teach the children about conservation and nature here in Florida. So don't tell me she received an anonymous donation."

Leah nodded. "I ran into her at the shop. She was telling me all about it. She said somebody dropped it off to her. It didn't even come in the mail."

"Neither did Mrs. Stoltzfus's," Hannah said with a frown. She drew her eyebrows together.

"Well, it seems your anonymous donor is going to great lengths not to be found if he's making sure the letters can't be traced," the rabbi said and picked up his steaming cup of coffee.

"You know what else that means," Jacob said and slipped to the edge of his seat. "It must be someone local. He must be a local if you can just walk up to people's mailboxes and drop off these checks."

"The first few did come by mail. Maybe he was mailing them at first and now decided to deliver in person. Anyhow, yes, so it's just a matter of time before we find out who he is," Leah agreed.

Hannah tapped her bottom lip. "I wonder if we could find out at the next community meeting. Maybe somebody will know."

"Or," the rabbi said after clearing his throat, "you could let him be. Or her. Them. Whoever it is."

"Let him be?" Hannah asked as though he'd spoken in another language.

The man sat down, his cup in his hands before him. "Well, it seems as though the person does not want to be found. As I said. From what I gather, donations appear where they are most needed and always appear in the form of cards with checks, none of which give away any identifying information."

Hannah swayed her head from side to side. "Well, yes, there never is any address or a name or anything."

"So why try to find out who it is?" the man asked. Leah was the one who spoke up next.

"But why not? He's doing a good deed, so he should be honored. Don't you agree? Shouldn't a good deed be rewarded? You have good deeds in your faith, surely," Leah asked.

The rabbi shrugged. "We have a great many mitzvot or, rather, good deeds. Charity is one of them. Let me ask you, are you familiar with Maimonides?"

Jacob, Leah, and Hannah exchanged glances, and each shrugged.

Rabbi Wise nodded. "Well, I didn't expect you to. He was one of the Jewish sages of old. And he spoke of charity at great length. So much so that today we use something called Maimonides' Ladder of Tzedakah, or Ladder of Charity. Essentially, the ladder has eight rungs. The lowest form of charity based on the ladder is occupied by one who gives begrudgingly and less than he can. The highest belongs to those people who enable a person to become self-sufficient so they no longer need charity. Through employment, for example." Hannah listened, quite fascinated by this.

"There are various steps on this ladder, but the third step is the one that concerns us. One of the highest in purest forms of charity is to give anonymously so that the person who received your gift does not feel obligated to repay it somehow. It is a charity given free of expectation. Truthfully I believe that is what the person donating is doing in your case. Otherwise, he would put his name on the checks. He wants to gift without his name being known because he does not want the recipients to feel they owe him anything. Would you really take this away from him if this is the case?"

Leah chewed on her bottom lip. Jacob sat with his arms crossed and tipped his head to one side. Hannah had never considered it possible that it was the kindest thing to let the anonymous donor do as he wished, help those in need without being recognized.

Rabbi Wise was not quite done with his lesson, either.

"Suppose I may use you as an example, Mrs. King. You have solved a great many mysteries over these past couple of years. Yet you never want to be thanked; you never want to be recognized or honored in any way. Why is that?"

"Because I think what I am doing is nothing special. I help people who need it. Sometimes, even when nobody asks me to do anything, I just stumble into the situation. None of it is of my doing. If we are going to be talking about the Lord coming out, then I will say that I suppose the Lord wants me to solve these mysteries. Therefore our glory is to be upon him and not me."

"What you are saying, Rabbi, is that our anonymous donor likely feels the same. He does not want to be recognized," Jacob chimed in.

The rabbi nodded and then finished his coffee. He set it down with a loud clang before getting up.

"That is true. I do not presume to know what his wants and needs are. Or hers, for that matter. All we know is that it could be a woman. It could be multiple people. In any case, we do not know what they want, but I say if they want to be recognized, they would've put their name down somewhere. If it were me, I would let them be." He glanced at the clock and rose. "Now, I must go. Otherwise, my arriving early on the plane will be for naught. I wish you all well." He tipped his head and left the room, leaving them alone.

As his footsteps faded away, Hannah looked from Jacob to Leah and back again when a thought came to her.

Perhaps this was a mystery that did not need to be solved.

Chapter Nine

The following week passed similarly to the last few. Again, donations appeared either in the form of checks or larger orders for the nursing home, school, or daycare.

Isaac continued to slip away to meet with Amanda while pretending to go to his charity event while the countdown to the deadline she'd given him continued to tick away.

And Susan? Well, Susan had taken Hannah's advice and taken to having coffee with Mr. Ivan Leroy. She'd seen them twice outside of Peterheims', looking contented. If this would turn into more than a friendship remained to be seen, but the smile on Susan's face did indicate as much.

Hannah sat in the community room that Wednesday with Jacob on her right. Leah and Lucas were on her left. The community room was packed. Since the start of the season, many people had returned to town, and this was the first community meeting since the beginning of the busy portion of the year.

It had been a long one. First, there had been singing, which was always pleasurable. Then they had prayed, a tranquil affair as always, but that had been followed by a less-than-tranquil debate.

Various people had put their names forth to become the next deacon, but in the end, it had been settled in a way that pleased everyone. Nobody presently in Pinecraft would be the deacon. Instead, they would reach out to the higher-ups in their church to have somebody assigned. It secmed safer that way. There was too much rivalry and ill will in their community now between those who wanted to retreat to the practices of old and those who were happy with the way things were.

Hannah had noticed that none of the Peterheims were there. News that they were selling their bakery had spread around Pinecraft, and it was now becoming clear that they were really leaving. They no longer had any vested interest in the community.

Hannah glanced at Isaac, who was seated beside Jacob. The young man turned his head, and they looked at one another, the quiet looks loaded down with heavy meaning

She thought back to the conversation and his confession, and as she peeked at

Jacob, she knew that soon her beloved fiancé's life would change. She knew she had to tell him, prepare him somehow, but she didn't know how.

Isaac would have to tell him within the next few days because the ultimatum she had given him was nearing its end.

Jacob looked at her and smiled, following up his expression with a wink. Hannah gulped, forced a smile and looked away, determined to push her family drama out of her mind for now.

At the front of the community space, the small woven basket into which they usually placed donations was being pulled out of the cabinet. Swiftly, it was making its way around the room. As it passed her, she put a few dollars inside when a plain-looking piece of paper caught her eye. This was unusual. People did not generally put checks into the basket. Without thinking, she reached into the basket, looking left and right because she was fully aware that this was not an acceptable thing to do, and then fished out the paper.

Beside her, Leah frowned, but when she saw what Hannah was holding, she shifted her body to shield her sister from view. Hannah quickly unfolded the paper and realized it was precisely what she had thought it was. A check.

"Well, would you look at this?" she mumbled as Jacob, Isaac, and Leah all bent over to take a better look at the check while Lucas looked around the room to make sure nobody noticed their actions.

It was a check made out to the Amish community of Pinecraft in the amount of

$20,000. Leah gasped and clasped one hand in front of her mouth to keep from drawing too much attention. Hannah discreetly flipped the check back into the basket and passed it on.

She looked around the room, wondering which of the people had placed the check in the basket when Rabbi Wise's words came back to her mind. She really should leave it alone, and yet the curious part of her that had been drawn into all of these mysteries over the past couple of years reared its head. She looked around the community room with a keen eye. Then, she recognized a familiar face seated at the other end of the aisle from her. The man, whose face she had not seen in almost two years, met her eyes before quickly getting up and slipping out.

"Excuse me," she whispered to Jacob and hurriedly made her way outside.

The tall and burly man had put on a long black coat and was rushing up the steps from the community room.

"Bontrager? Arthur Bontrager?" she called out. The man stopped midway up the steps, and she saw his hand tightening around the railing. He glanced over his shoulder and let out a deep breath of air.

"I should have known coming here was a bad idea." He turned, and for the first time in two years, Hannah got a good look at the man who had done all he could to vandalize their community out of anger at being shunned by his own community years ago.

"What are you doing here, Mr. Bontrager?" Hannah asked as she walked toward him.

He shrugged. "You know very well what I'm doing. I'm spreading my wealth to those who can use it to do some actual good. Your check is coming, by the way. I was saving you for last."

Hannah did not quite know what to say. The very first mystery she had ever solved was the one of the Amish vandal. A man had vandalized many of the businesses in the area, causing tension between the English world, whom they had suspected of the misdeeds. When it was revealed that a former Amish man had committed the acts, the shock had vibrated throughout the community. But in the end, it had brought them closer together.

Not much of that closeness was left due to the past few weeks' events.

Arthur Bontrager had escaped legal punishment after coming to an agreement with the community. He had paid for the damages he had caused, made a donation, and then left, agreeing never to return. And yet here he was.

"Mr. Bontrager, I don't understand. Why are you here giving away your wealth?"

He lowered himself onto the steps leading up. He supported his arms by placing them on his legs and dropped his head between his shoulders. As he sat that way, Hannah noticed that he had lost weight. His cheeks were gaunt beneath his shaggy beard, and she could see the outline of his collar bones beneath his button-down blue checkered shirt.

"Mrs. King, I am dying. I've got a few weeks left."

"Oh, Mr. Bontrager. I am so sorry to hear that," Hannah gasped and clasped her hand in front of her face.

"Are you really? You sound almost like you actually do mean it," he scoffed but met her eye and held her stare

"Of course I mean it. It is awful. I never wish anything bad on anybody. You paid your dues, and you made it right with us. Even if you hadn't, I wouldn't wish you... this."

He sighed. "And that is why I came back here. Your community was so forgiving of me even though I was awful, and I treated you all terribly. Even though none of you were involved in my shunning. When the doctor told me that the end was near, I sat down with my accountant and made my will. I'm leaving most of my money to charity. I don't have much family to speak of, and I know it's petty, but I don't want the people who shunned me to get any of it. I thought I would have some peace of mind by giving everything to charity, but I didn't. I kept thinking back to you all, the people of Pinecraft. You could've sent me to jail, and you didn't. So I thought to myself, What better place to leave some of my wealth than Pinecraft?"

"Oh, Mr. Bontrager, I wish this was still the Pinecraft you knew. But, I'm afraid things aren't quite…"

He raised his hand, silencing her. "I am well aware. I did not become rich by being a fool. I know things are changing here. That is part of why I chose to give, and to the people I have given to." He smiled before continuing on. "All the people who received an anonymous donation want to make Pinecraft better, want to keep it open and welcoming. People like you."

"But why didn't you sign the checks? People would think very highly of you for doing this."

He grimaced. "I am not doing this for the recognition. I'm doing it for the greater good. And I would really appreciate it if you didn't tell anybody that it was me making the donations. Let me slip away into the night, get back into my car and drive back home to my little cottage in Key West. Let me die knowing that I've done something good to the people I've wronged, and I've done it in a way that needs no thanks. Do you think you can do that for me?"

Hannah swallowed hard but then nodded. She wasn't sure why, but something in the way Mr. Bontrager had made his request had touched her; indeed, it had almost moved her to tears. This was a man who knew he was dying, and his last wish on his earth was to do something good, something that would last, something for others. She nodded once, and then he heaved himself up and stopped to catch his breath.

"I thank you. You're a good woman. I wish nothing but blessings upon you and your family."

He turned and made his way up the steps when Hannah stepped forward.

"Mr. Bontrager, would you wait a moment?"

He stopped and looked over his shoulder. "Of course. What is it, Mrs. King?"

"My family, I feel we are about to encounter a situation that is not unlike the one you faced."

He looked at her for a long moment. "I heard rumors about your son and the Bailey girl. You fear that if he goes back to her, you'll have to shun him like my family shunned me. Let me give you a piece of advice, Mrs. King. Whatever happens, you must do what you think is right. That is a decision that is going to be between you and your husband and the Lord. No matter what the community tells you, those are the people that matter. And another piece of advice I have for you is this, do not ever allow anger to eat its way into your heart. It will lead only to bitterness. Now, God bless you and yours."

And with that, Mr. Bontrager, the Amish vandal, walked away for the last time, leaving Hannah to stand on her own with the weight of the world on her shoulders once more.

From inside the community hall came the sound of chairs shuffling. And then, the door opened, and her family poured out, their faces marked with questions.

"Did you find out who the donor was?" Leah asked urgently as Hannah took Jacob's hand. Isaac stepped out beside him, a curious expression on his face.

"I did, and I have to say, Rabbi Wise was right indeed. The donor wants to stay anonymous, and I think we ought to let him."

Leah let out a dramatic sigh. "Very well, Hannah. Have it your way. I suppose as long as it all goes toward something good, that's all that matters."

Hannah squeezed Jacob's hand and then, with Isaac beside them, they walked up the steps out into the cool evening air. As they passed the bakery, they spotted Susan sitting there with Ivan Leroy.

"Hannah, Jacob! Join us," she called. Hannah looked at Jacob, who winked at her.

"I think we ought to. That is a story I'd like to hear in more detail," he said.

Hannah squeezed his hand and decided that, for the moment, she would put her worries aside and join in the joy that radiated from her friend Susan. There would be opportunity to solve her own troubles another time.

For now, it was time to do what she loved best: spend time with the people she loved.

The End

FREE GIFT

Just to say thanks for checking our works we like to gift you

Our Exclusive Never Before Released Books

100% FREE!

Please GO TO

http://cleanromancepublishing.com/gift

And get your FREE gift

Thanks for being such a wonderful client.

Please Check out My Other Works

By checking out the link below

http://cleanromancepublishing.com/rbauth

Thank You

Many thanks for taking the time to buy and read through this book.

It means lots to be supported by SPECIAL readers like YOU.

Hope you enjoyed the book; please support my writing by leaving an honest review to assist other readers.

.

With Regards,

Ruth Bawell

Printed in Great Britain
by Amazon

23955009R00071